TOBY
THE GOPHER TURTLE

BY BETH CLARK
ILLUSTRATED BY JASON VELAZQUEZ

Toby the Gopher Turtle
© 2020 by Beth Clark
Illustrated by Jason Velazquez

Printed in the United States of America.
ISBN-13: 978-0-5787245-3-9
LCCN: 2020912353

Beth Books
Blackshear, Georgia

beth
BOOKS

Meet Toby. Toby is a gopher turtle. Toby loves to dig burrows. He has special feet that act like shovels.

Here is Toby's home. He dug this burrow all by himself.

Toby is at the beach. He made himself a beach home with a beautiful view of the ocean.

Toby has a friend visiting. He sometimes uses Toby's burrow as a temporary home.

Toby is taking care of some of his eggs.
Look! The babies are coming out now!

Toby likes to make sure he burrows around the tall grass and plants, so the babies are protected.

Toby is taking a break from digging. He goes closer to the ocean to see the people. Toby hides behind the grass and sees a child building a sandcastle.

Toby grabs a snack before going to see some friends. Toby loves to eat grass and flowers nearby. YUM!

Look! It's Cari the Crab! Cari is an ocean friend of Toby's. Cari invites Toby to a swim party. He would love to go, but Toby isn't so sure. Toby's feet are great for digging burrows, but not so great for swimming.

Toby gives thought to the invitation, unsure about the swim party. But he decides to go anyway. Toby gets to the edge of the water and sees his friends.

The waves begin to rush over Toby. It's so refreshing! Time to jump in!

Toby gets in the water. The water currents sweep Toby deeper into the ocean. As the water whooshes Toby upside down and right side up, his friends try to help.

Sarah the Sea Turtle sees Toby. She rushes over to help him.

Toby is sad because he cannot swim very well. Sarah tells Toby why his feet cannot swim like hers. Toby's feet are special in their own way. They were made to dig burrows. These burrows are super special. They create a home, not only for Toby, but for his friends too.

Sarah helps Toby back to the beach. Toby is so happy his feet are special in their own way. They might not be great for swimming, but they can make burrows. Not just for him, but his friends too!

As the sun begins to set, Toby will sometimes go to the edge of the ocean to see his swimming friends.

And when the sun goes to bed, so does Toby, in his cozy little burrow he dug all by himself. Goodnight!

About
TOBY
THE GOPHER TURTLE

Gopher turtles are reptiles who love to dig deep burrows as their home. Gopher turtles are not meant to be great swimmers, but they are amazing diggers. They share their burrows with many other animals, including mice, snakes, rabbits, frogs, foxes, and even some bugs. For this reason, the gopher turtle is a very important contributor to the ecosystem.

This reptile can live for up to 60 years in the wild, although there are records of gopher turtles living up to 90 years in captivity. You can find these amazing reptiles in Florida and the southern most parts of Alabama, Georgia, and South Carolina.

You can make a donation to support the gopher turtle and other amazing wildlife to the National Wildlife Federation by visiting:

https://support.nwf.org/page/9384/donate/

Also by Beth Clark

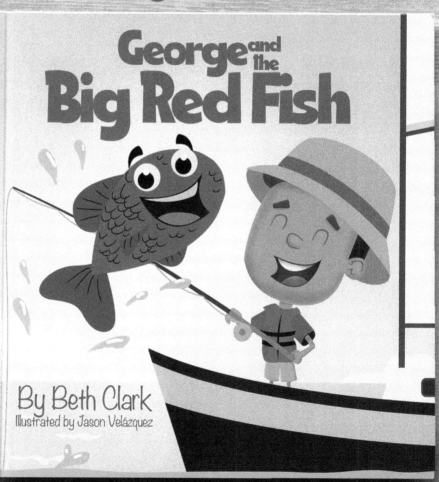

George and the
Big Red Fish

By Beth Clark

Illustrated by Jason Velázquez

CPSIA information can be obtained
at www.ICGtesting.com
Printed in the USA
LVHW070855110723
751984LV00005B/20